This book is given with love

To:

From:

About the Author

Dr. Daniela Owen is a psychologist who brings to life healthy mind concepts and strategies for children everywhere. For more about the author please check out

drdanielaowen.com

For Lila Skye

 Published in the United States
by Puppy Dogs & Ice Cream, Inc.
ISBN:978-1-955151-29-0
Edition: May 2021

For all inquiries, please contact us at:
info@puppysmiles.org

To see more of our books, visit us at:
www.PuppyDogsAndIceCream.com

EVERYONE FEELS ANGRY SOMETIMES

Written by:
Dr. Daniela Owen

Illustrated by:
Gülce Baycik

Anger is a ***BIG*** feeling.

We can feel angry when
we don’t get what we want,
when something isn’t fair,
or when we have to do things
we don’t want to do.

I WANT IT!
No.

Anger starts deep inside of us...

and grows and grows.

ANGER
ANGER
ANGER
ANGER
ANGER

Even though it doesn’t feel good,
it’s okay to feel angry.

Everyone feels angry sometimes...

But when our anger gets too ***BIG***,
it explodes out of us!

In fact, anger is like lava, and
our bodies are like volcanoes.

When we are calm, the anger stays inside of our volcanoes.

When we are calm, our volcanoes are cool and inactive.

But when we get really angry,
these feelings come bursting out,
hot and destructive.

This can make us feel out of control,
like an erupting volcano.

When our volcanoes explode,
we may stomp our feet,
pound our fists,
kick, scream and yell,
throw things, rip things,
and break things.

Sound familiar?

NOT FAIR!

It’s helpful to think about
our anger in 4 levels.

***Low, medium, high,
and exploding.***

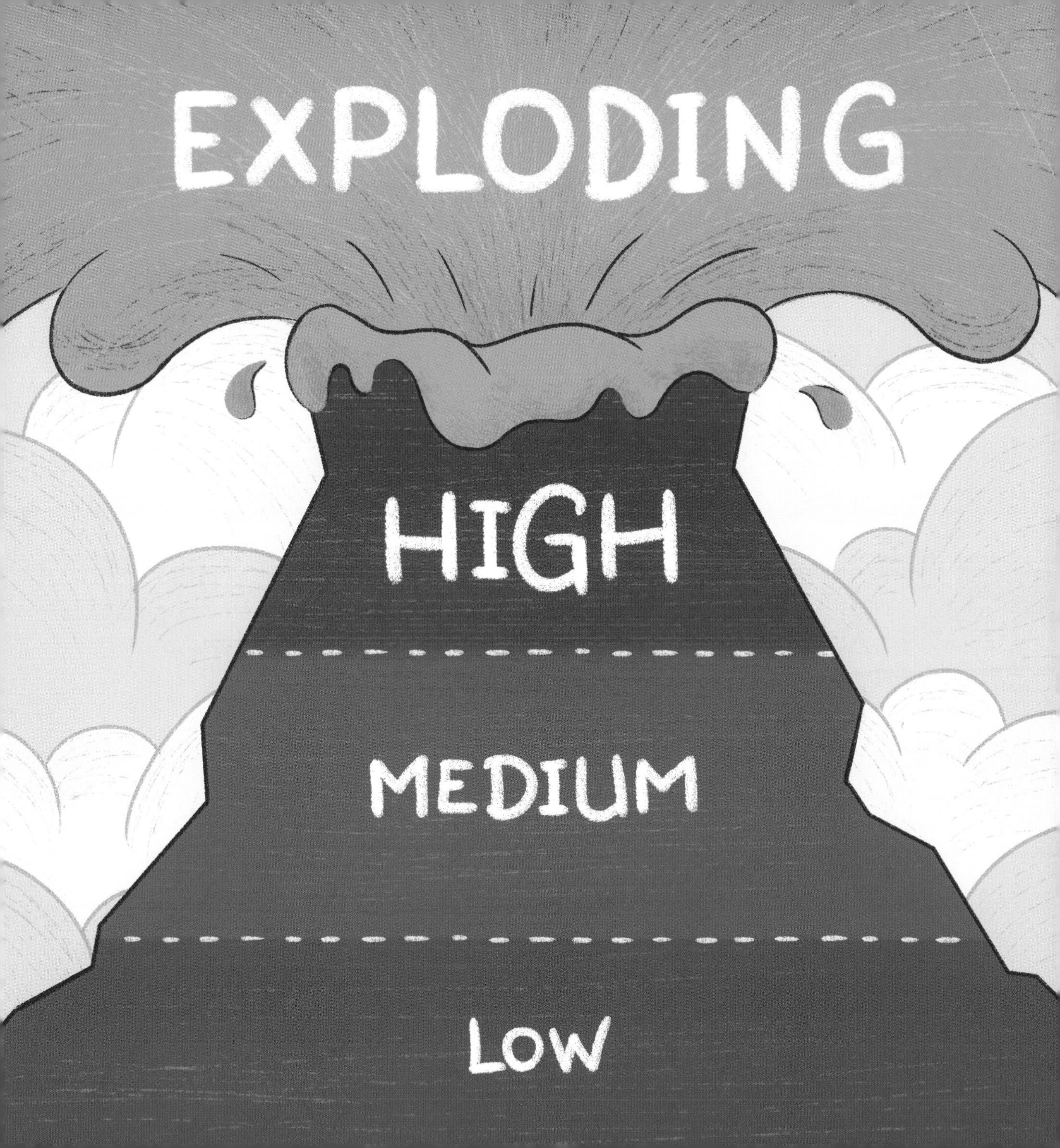

EXPLODING

HIGH

MEDIUM

LOW

When we feel calm,
our bodies are relaxed.

We speak at a normal volume and
our thoughts are clear in our heads.

Our anger level is ***low.***

When we get a little angry,
our bodies start to feel tense.

Our voices get louder or faster.
Our thoughts start to speed up
and become focused on the
thing that is bothering us.

Our anger level is ***medium.***

When we get angrier,
our bodies and faces feel warm.

Our hands become fists.
Our voices get louder.

We repeat the same thing again
and again. Our thoughts become
focused on what's making us angry.

Our anger level is ***high.***

When we get the angriest,
our faces and bodies feel hot and tight.

Our voices yell or scream.
Our thoughts get jumbled in our heads,
and we usually can't focus on
anything at all.

Our anger level is ***exploding!***

But the good news is...
there are steps you can take to
control your anger volcano.

Step 1:

Notice your lava level.
Are your cheeks getting warm?
Are your hands forming fists?

Do you feel like you could scream?
Your lava is heating up!

It's time for Step 2.

Step 2:

Clasp your hands behind your back.

Take 10 steps away from the situation or person who is making you angry.

1... 2...
3... 4... 5...
6... 7... 8...
1
2
3
4
5
6
7
8

Step 3:

Take ***10*** slow, deep breaths.
Breathe in slowly,
then breathe out slowly.

Count each breath,
until you finish all ten.

IN

OUT

IN

OUT

IN

OUT

Step 4:

Move your body!
Moving our bodies in non-angry
ways helps us release anger.

Do 25 jumping jacks.
Run up and down stairs.
Do 10 cartwheels or somersaults.
Put on some music and dance around.

It doesn’t matter what you do,
as long as you move your body a lot.

It's always a good idea to take a break from whatever is making you angry.

If it's a person, tell them that you'll talk to them later.

If it's a game or activity, stop doing it for now. You can finish playing later.

It doesn't have to be a long break, just long enough for you to ***calm*** your anger volcano.

We often feel angry when
something seems unfair.

If we continue to focus
on the unfair thing,
our anger and jealousy
will ***grow and grow.***

But if we choose to think about
something positive instead,
our anger will get ***smaller and smaller.***

HIGH SCORE!
6,000,000
YOU ARE A
WINNER!

Once you practice these steps a few times,
you will start to feel ***more and more***
in control of your anger volcano.

Calm... Calm...

Being able to control our anger
makes us feel good!

Remember...
Everyone feels angry sometimes!

Steps to Calm Down

Step 1:
Notice your lava level.

Step 2:
Take 10 steps away from the situation.

Step 3:
Take 10, slow deep breaths.
Step 4:
Move your body! Movement helps release anger from our bodies.

Thank you for purchasing

Everyone Feels Angry Sometimes,

and welcome to the Puppy Dogs & Ice Cream family.

We're certain you're going to love the little gift
we've prepared for you at the website above.